I Will RACE You Through This Book!

To all my running friends. Thank you for the happy miles!—JF

PENGUIN WORKSHOP
An Imprint of Penguin Random House LLC, New York

Copyright © 2019 by Jonathan Fenske. All rights reserved. Published by Penguin Workshop, an imprint of Penguin Random House LLC, New York. PENGUIN and PENGUIN WORKSHOP are trademarks of Penguin Books Ltd, and the W colophon is a registered trademark of Penguin Random House LLC. Manufactured in China.

Visit us online at www.penguinrandomhouse.com.

Library of Congress Cataloging-in-Publication Data is available upon request.

ISBN 9781524791957   10 9 8 7 6 5 4 3 2 1

I Will RACE You Through This Book!

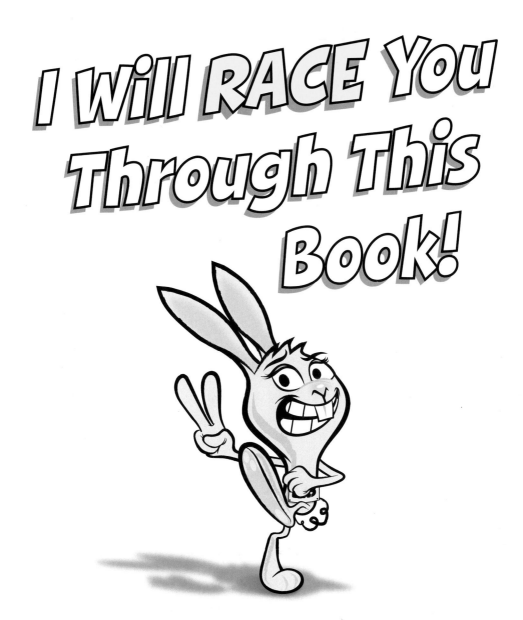

by Jonathan Fenske

Penguin Workshop

4

I am

BOOK-IT BUNNY,

see?

**No one reads
as fast as
ME!**

So turn the page
and take a look.

I will RACE you
through this book!

Readers, on your mark!
GET SET!

Now
CLOSE
YOUR
EYES

and

DO
NOT
PEEK.

9

What?
I would not
EVER
sneak!

Please be a pal and wait for me!

Get ready! I will count to THREE.

ONE... TWO...

13

THR

SLOW DOWN!

I need to get some

You LOOKED, and I am winning now!

It **IS** a flying cow.
Oh, wow!

Uh-oh!
I see
THE END
is near.

And you
are reading
FAST!
Oh dear!

If only
I could
S T R E T C H
an ear . . .

THE END
(KIND OF)

PLOP!

I guess you beat me by a HAIR.

So what? Big deal? Why should I CARE?

I am HAPPY. See my grin?

27

I did not even **WANT** to win.

Now run along.
You won.
Good day.

Go find another place to play.

I will find more
books to read,

and wow SOMEBODY
with my speed!

Hello, SNAIL!
I like your look!

I will race
YOU through
this book!